Copyright © 2003 by Nord-Süd Verlag AG, Gossau Zürich, Switzerland
First published in Switzerland under the title *Wach auf, kleiner Bär, Weihnachten ist da!*
English translation copyright © 2003 by North-South Books Inc., New York

All rights reserved. No part of this book may be reproduced or utilized
in any form or by any means, electronic or mechanical, including photocopying,
recording, or any information storage and retrieval system,
without permission in writing from the publisher.

First published in Great Britain in 2003 by North-South Books,
an imprint of Nord-Süd Verlag AG, Gossau Zürich, Switzerland.

First published in the United States, Canada, Australia,
and New Zealand in 2004 by North-South Books, an imprint
of Nord-Süd Verlag AG, Gossau Zürich, Switzerland.

Distributed in the United States by North-South Books Inc., New York.

Library of Congress Cataloging-in-Publication Data is available.
A CIP catalogue record for this book is available from The British Library.
ISBN 0-7358-1851-7 (trade edition)
1 3 5 7 9 HC 10 8 6 4 2
ISBN 0-7358-1852-5 (library edition)
1 3 5 7 9 LE 10 8 6 4 2
Printed in Germany

For more information about our books, and the authors and artists
who create them, visit our web site: www.northsouth.com

Sleepy Bear's Christmas

By **Udo Weigelt**

Illustrated by **Cristina Kadmon**

Translated by J. Alison James

North-South Books
New York / London

Spring had come. The snow and ice had melted. The sun was shining and it was warm again at last. Baby Bear crawled from his cave and saw the world for the first time.

"You're new, aren't you?" chittered Squirrel. "I didn't see you the last time all the animals got together."

"When was that?" asked Baby Bear.

"Christmas!" said Squirrel.

"Christmas?" asked Baby Bear. "What is Christmas?"

Squirrel closed her eyes and smiled. "Christmas is when the snow is falling, but our coats keep us warm, and everyone is jolly and we sing all day long."

"That sounds lovely," said Baby Bear.

"Were you at Christmas?" Baby Bear asked Hare.

Hare, as usual, was in a hurry. "Yup! Yup! Yup!" he said.

"What happened?" asked Baby Bear.

"We gave nice presents to each other," Hare said, and he bounced away.

Presents, thought Baby Bear. Presents would be nice.

When Baby Bear met Beaver he asked her about Christmas.

"Oh, you are a young thing, aren't you," Beaver said fondly. "The part of Christmas I like best is when we gather together to tell stories. I like the one about the reindeer from the far North who fly through the woods, leaving no tracks behind them."

"How can that be?" asked Baby Bear.

"You don't have to understand stories for them to be wonderful," Beaver explained.

Baby Bear went to Mother Bear.

"How long is it until Christmas?" he asked. "I can't
wait for the songs and the stories and the presents!"

"Oh, sweet little bear," Mother Bear said gently, "we sleep
through the winter. Bears can never have Christmas,
because we are dreaming in our caves. That is just the
way it is, and we can't change it."

Baby Bear met Hedgehog. "Did you know that bears sleep all winter?" he asked. "We sleep right through Christmas. Isn't that awful?"

Hedgehog flicked his prickers and nodded. "We do, too. But we make up for it in the summer. We have a Hedgefest. Do you want to come? You'd be welcome, if you didn't eat too many berries."

"No," Baby Bear said, "but thank you for asking me."

Baby Bear spent the rest of the summer, and most of the autumn, too, asking questions about Christmas. He wanted to know every story. He wanted to know every song. He wanted to know what presents the animals were getting for one another.

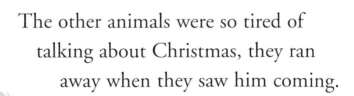

The other animals were so tired of talking about Christmas, they ran away when they saw him coming.

"Do you know what, Baby Bear?" Mother Bear said at last. "Bears can't celebrate Christmas because of our winter sleep. But by now you have found out so much about Christmas that you will surely dream about it. And that is better than nothing!"

Baby Bear supposed it would have to be.

The wind blew cold, and Baby Bear's breath
steamed around his nose. The trees lost their leaves,
and there was frost in the air. Baby Bear was full of berries
and honey and very, very tired. He curled up next to his
mother in their bear cave.

Baby Bear thought and thought about Christmas.
He remembered everything the animals had said, all
the stories and all the songs . . . and he fell deeply asleep.

Baby Bear *did* dream about Christmas—Christmas
in his bear cave. All the animals gathered, and there were
presents for everyone. A strange glowing light fell around
them, and then they were dancing, and someone was
shaking Baby Bear . . . and shaking him . . .

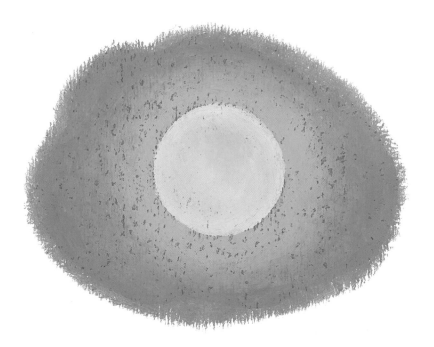

. . . until Baby Bear woke up.

The forest animals really *were* there! Even Mother Bear and Hedgehog were awake. Mother Bear took Baby Bear in her arms. They were both terribly sleepy, but they sang songs with the animals. Then they listened to stories, and everyone opened a present.

The glowing light was all around their warm and happy faces. Baby Bear rubbed his eyes and wondered at the beauty of it all.

When the animals had all gone home, Mother Bear
nuzzled Baby Bear. "Now you have had your Christmas,"
she said, "and you can remember it for the rest of your life."

Baby Bear sighed with pleasure. "It was even more lovely
than I had imagined," he said sleepily.

Baby Bear snuggled into Mother Bear and went to sleep.
Soon he was dreaming again, but not of Christmas.
Now he dreamed of Squirrel and Hedgehog, of Hare
and Beaver.

And of springtime.